Winter Magic

BY EVELINE HASLER
ILLUSTRATED BY MICHÈLE LEMIEUX

KIDS CAN PRESS LTD.
TORONTO

Printed by permission of Otto Maier Verlag, Germany

First Canadian edition published August 1989

CANADIAN CATALOGUING IN PUBLICATION DATA

Hasler, Eveline
  Winter magic

Translation of: Im Winterland.
ISBN 0-921103-71-9

I. Lemieux, Michèle.   II. Title.

PZ7.H2765Wi 1989   j833′.914   C89-094310-9

With kind appreciation to Morrow Junior Books, William Morrow
and Company, Inc., New York for their help in the production of the
Canadian edition.

Printed and bound in Hong Kong by Wing King Tong Company Limited

89 0 9 8 7 6 5 4 3 2

Winter Magic

Peter and Sebastian the cat sit in the window watching the snow. "The grass is gone. The animals are gone. There's nothing but snow," says Peter. "I hate winter."

Peter's mother calls him for dinner. "Eat your soup," she says, "before it gets cold. After dinner it will be story time."

Mother tells a story about the winter king and the animals of his icicle kingdom: Rabbit, Fox, Bird, Badger, and Mouse.

Soon Peter is off to bed. His blanket
feels warm and fluffy. Peter dreams his
bed is a cloud flying over the snow forest.

Sebastian is in the forest.
Peter dances with the animals
of the icicle kingdom.

Suddenly Peter sits up in bed.
Sebastian is out in the forest, thinks
Peter. He could be freezing in the winter
night.

But he's not. He's safe and warm in
the drawer of Mother's china cabinet.
"Sebastian," says Peter, "my eyes must
be playing tricks. I saw you dancing in
the snow forest."

"Winter is full of secrets," says Sebastian. "But you need the right kind of eyes to see them."

"What kind of eyes?" asks Peter.

"Eyes like mine," says Sebastian. "Now get ready."

"Where are we going?" asks Peter.

"To the winterland," says Sebastian, "to look for its secrets." With every word Sebastian grows larger. "Hop on my back," he says, "and we're off."

With Peter on his back, Sebastian jumps through the snow. Sometimes they sink deep into the white waves.

"Where is everything?" asks Peter. "All I can see is snow."

"Help me dig the snow away from this tree," says Sebastian, "and you'll see one of winter's secrets."

They burrow deep under the tree. "Here are the roots that store the tree's food," says Sebastian. "In the winter, everything happens underground. In the spring, the leaves will grow again."

"Look," says Peter, "here's where the mice have disappeared to. They've made a winter home under the roots. They are eating the nuts and seeds they have stored here."

"I'm very hungry myself," says Sebastian, licking his whiskers.

"Do you see that badger? Badgers sleep underground all winter. During their long winter sleep they don't have to eat at all."

"The badger is smiling in his sleep," says Peter. "I think he is dreaming about the spring."

"Let's not wake him," says Sebastian. "It's time to travel on."

"Why can't the fox sleep?" asks Peter.

"He has to hunt," says Sebastian. "He's hungry all year long."

"It's stopped snowing," says Peter.
"It's so quiet I can hear the birds
rustling their feathers."

"It's easier to hear in the winter,"
says Sebastian.

"Is this a magic forest?" asks Peter.
"I think I see elves hiding in the trees."

"It's just the ice on the branches,"
says Sebastian. "Everything looks different
in wintertime."

As they ride on, the day begins to break. Sebastian shows Peter an ice cave. As the sun rises, the icicles shimmer and glow.

"Does the winter king live here?" asks Peter.

"The winter king lives everywhere," says Sebastian.

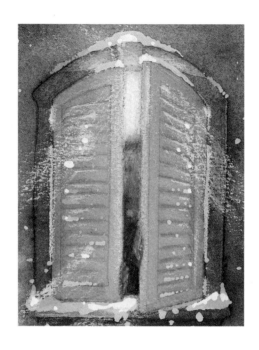

"I like winter," says Peter.
"But I'm glad to be getting home."
"In the winter," says Sebastian,
"there's no place like home."

Eveline Hasler was born in Switzerland and studied in Paris and Freiburg, West Germany. She is the author of many books for adults and children and a writer for Swiss and German television. Her stories have been translated into Italian, Spanish, Dutch, French, and Japanese, and in 1976 she was awarded the Hans Christian Andersen Certificate of Honor. Eveline Hasler lives in Switzerland with her husband and three children.

Michèle Lemieux was born in Quebec. She has lived and worked as an illustrator of books and magazines in Paris, Montreal, Toronto, and Freiburg, West Germany. *What's That Noise?* a story she both wrote and illustrated, was her first book published in the United States. Michèle Lemieux lives in Montreal.